Dizzy
and the Talkie-Talkie

Scrambler
and the Off-road Race

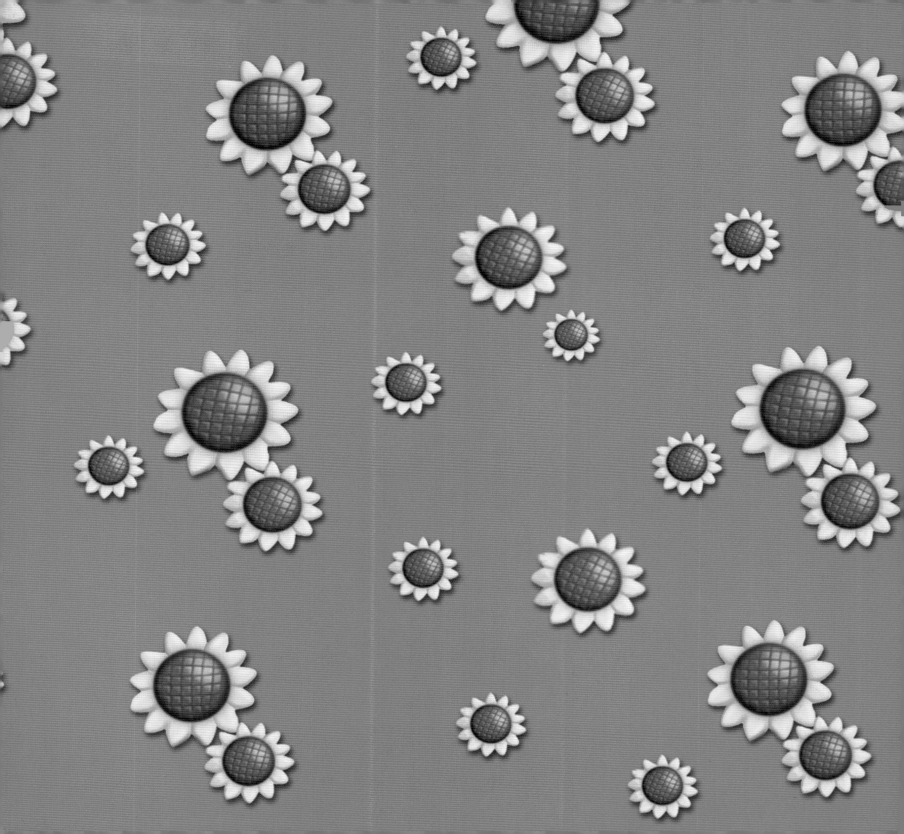

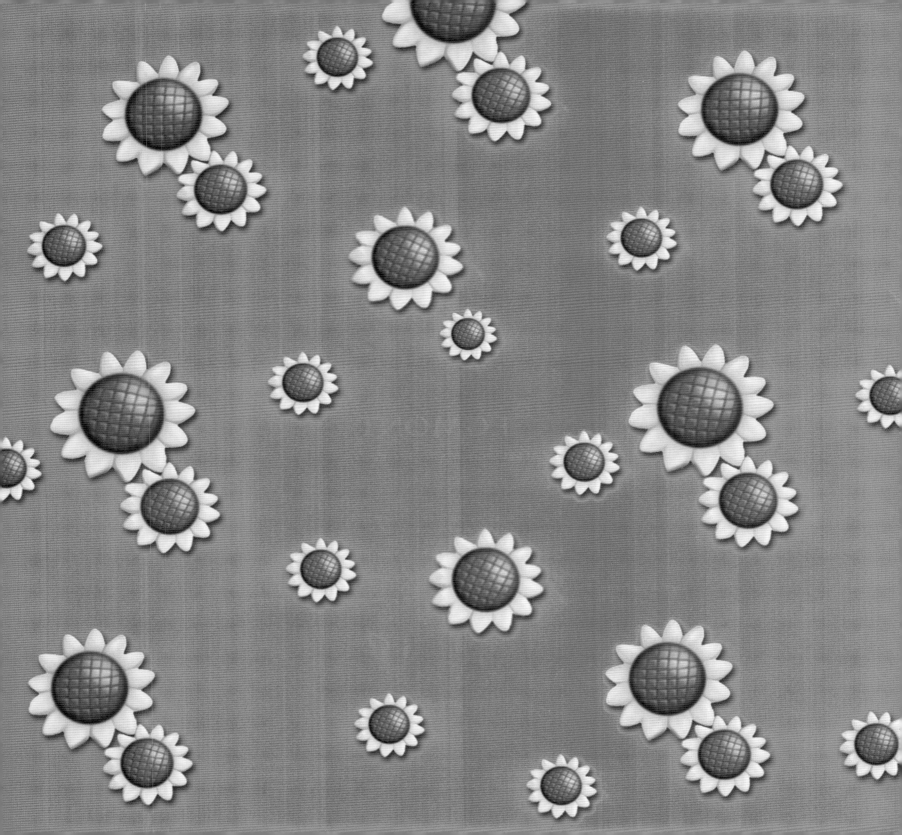

EGMONT

We bring stories to life

This edition published for BCA in 2008
First published in Great Britain 2007
by Egmont UK Limited,
239 Kensington High Street, London W8 6SA

HiT entertainment

ISBN 978 0 6035 6379 9

1 3 5 7 9 10 8 6 4 2
Printed in Italy

CONTENTS

Dizzy
and the Talkie-Talkie

Scrambler
and the Off-road Race

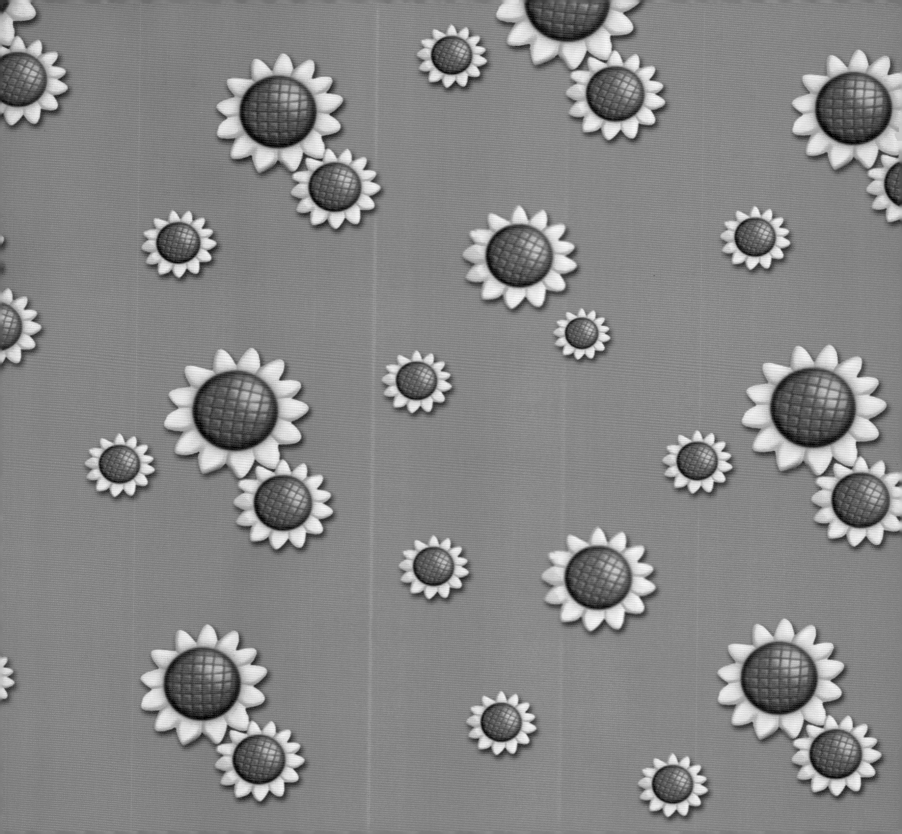

Dizzy
and the Talkie-Talkie

Illustrations by Craig Cameron

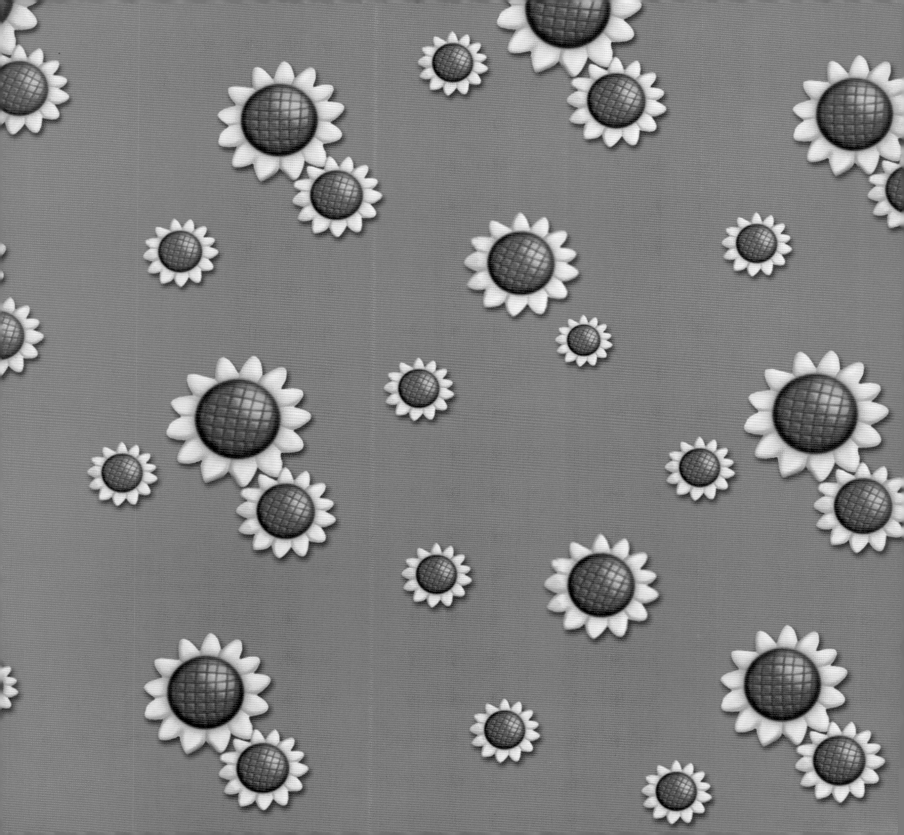

When Wendy brings the talkie-talkies to Sunflower Valley the machines have lots of fun with them. But Dizzy soon finds out how helpful they can be . . .

One sunny morning, Bob and the team were gathered around a large metal tank in the new yard in Sunflower Valley.

"This will be our new water tank," Bob told the machines. "We can use it to store our water. We will pump the water from the ground through the pipes using a hand pump."

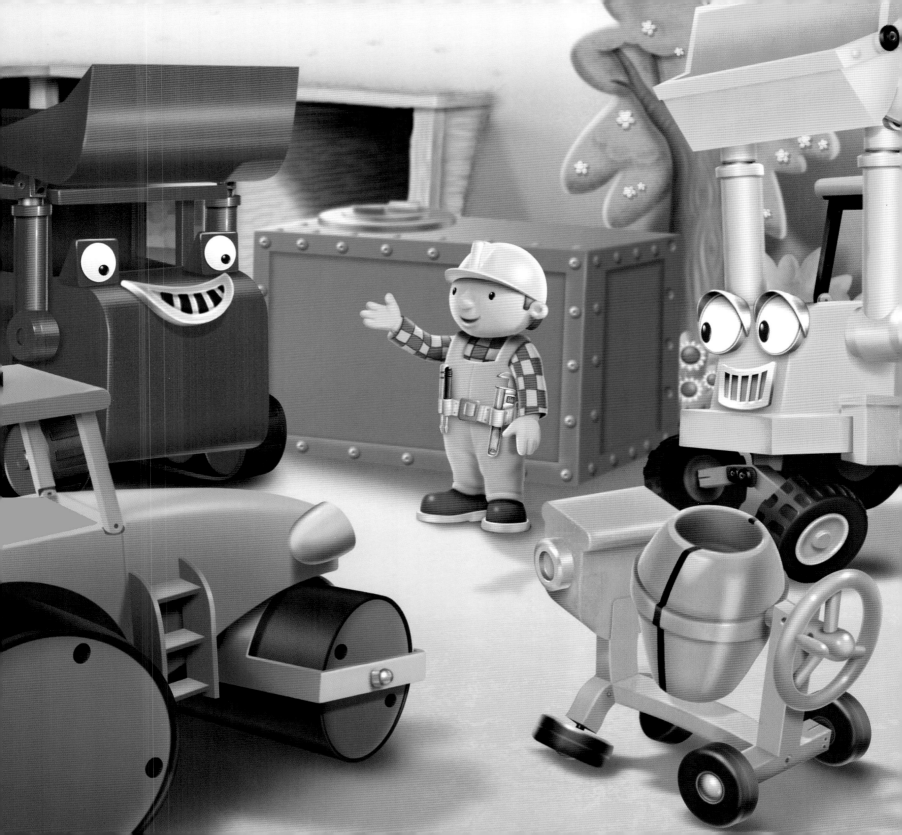

"Hello, everyone!" called Wendy driving in to the yard on Scrambler.

"I've got a present for each of you. They're called talkie-talkies! You can use the headsets to talk to each other wherever you are in Sunflower Valley!" said Wendy, as she handed out the headsets.

"Rock and roll!" smiled Roley.

"That reminds me," said Bob. "We still need some rocks for the tank."

"Dizzy and I can go and find rocks," suggested Scrambler. "We can use the talkie-talkies to let Muck know when we find some. Let's scram!"

"Remember your way so you can get back," called Wendy, as they left.

"OK team? Can we build it?" Bob asked.

"Yes we can!" everyone cheered.

"Then let's get started! Lofty, you will be getting soil out using this special drill so we can reach the water."

"OK, Bob," said Lofty, and he got to work.

"Dizzy to Scrambler! Can you hear me?"
asked Dizzy.

The friends were having fun using the talkie-talkies!

"Cor, look at that big boulder," said Scrambler.
"We won't forget we passed that!"

Dizzy and Scrambler came to a sudden stop.
There had been a landslide and the path was
blocked with rocks!

Dizzy called Muck to tell him they had found some rocks. Muck set off down the track that Dizzy and Scrambler had taken.

Very soon, Muck came to the big boulder. "Muck to Dizzy, which way do I go at the big boulder, please?" he asked, using his talkie-talkie.

"Erm, you turn left," Dizzy told Muck.

Muck carried on until he came to two trees that looked like an arch.

Dizzy couldn't remember seeing an arch.
"Go right, I think," said Dizzy.

"And where do I go at the woods?" asked Muck.

"Erm, I don't remember any woods," replied Dizzy.

"Oh, no!" cried Muck. "I'm lost!"

Dizzy had an idea. "What can you see around you?" she asked Muck.

"Erm, a big hill with a cloud on top," replied Muck.

"Cool as a mule, Muck! Coz I see the big hill with the cloud, too," added Scrambler, over his talkie-talkie. "Head for the hill and you should find us."

Dizzy and Scrambler were starting to wonder if Muck would ever find them when Muck appeared suddenly.

"Muck's on the job!" he grinned. "Let's load up those rocks and get them back to Bob."

"But we don't know how to get back," moaned Scrambler.

Dizzy remembered how Muck had found them.

"Dizzy to Roley," she whispered into the talkie-talkie. "What big things can you see?"

"A really tall tree, taller than all the others," Roley whispered back.

"Come on!" Dizzy told Roley and Muck. "Let's head for the really tall tree!"

Back at the yard, Bob was beginning to wonder where Dizzy, Scrambler and Muck had got to.

"Call them on the talkie-talkie base unit!" suggested Wendy.

"Bob to Dizzy!" Bob began.

"Dizzy to Bob!" came a voice right behind him. "We're back! And we've got rocks."

Soon the water tank was finished. Wendy tried the pump and the pipes began to rattle.

Splash! Water flew out of the pipes and soaked poor Bob!

"Dizzy to Bob," giggled Dizzy. "Hee, hee, you left the tap on!"

"Oh, Dizzy!" said Bob. And everybody began to laugh! It was another job well done for Bob and the machine team.

THE END

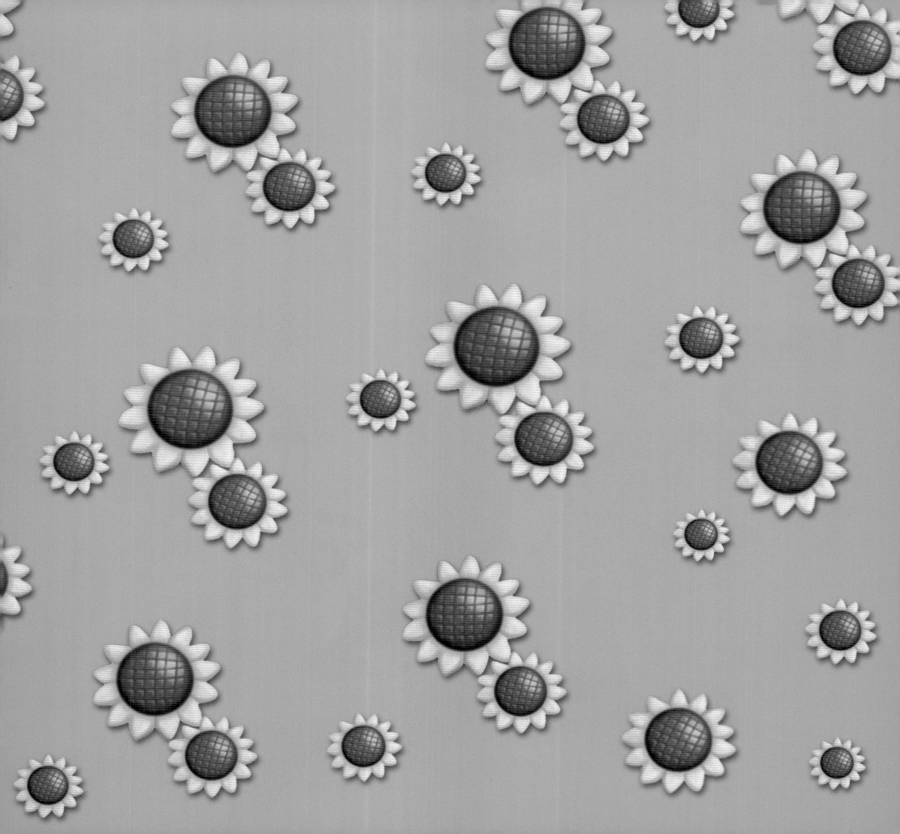

Scrambler
and the Off-road Race

Illustrations by Pulsar

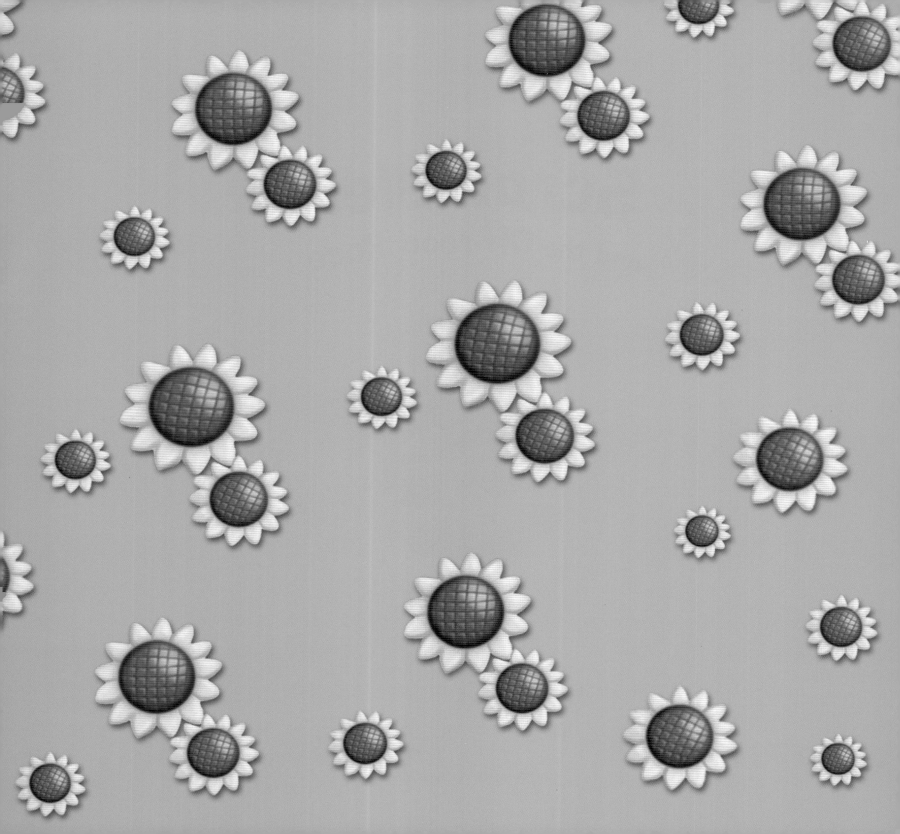

Scrambler really wants to help Bob in Sunflower Valley. But how can an off-road racer be useful on a building site?

It was a lovely day in Sunflower Valley, and the team had a new job.

"We're building a barn for Farmer Pickles!" announced Bob.

Scruffty was excited. "Ruff! Ruff!" he barked, as he raced around Bob's legs.

But Bob didn't have time to play.

Scrambler was excited, too. He really wanted to help Bob and Wendy.

"What will I be doing?" he asked.

Bob shook his head.

"I'm sorry, Scrambler," he said.
"But there isn't really a job for you to do."

Scrambler was disappointed. But then Bob had an idea.

"There is something you can do," smiled Bob. "You can take Scruffty for a walk!"

"But that's not a proper job," said Scrambler, sadly.

"Yes it is," replied Bob. "You'll be keeping Scruffty safe."

The whole team was excited about building
the barn.

"Can we build it?" Scoop asked.

"Yes we can!" the machines all cried.

"Er, yeah, I think so," added Lofty.

But poor Scrambler said nothing.
He trailed sadly off to walk Scruffty.

Scruffty ran on ahead, panting excitedly. "Ruff! Ruff!"

Scrambler followed slowly. He felt miserable.

"I can't believe I'm walking a dog!" he grumbled.
"I thought I was going to get something important
to do."

But when they got to the woods, Scrambler found he was starting to have fun with Scruffty. Especially when they played hide and seek!

When it was Scruffty's turn to hide, he ran off instead. The little dog didn't understand how to play the game!

Back at the site, everyone was working very hard.

Lofty was helping Bob and Wendy set up a wooden frame for the walls and roof of the barn.

Dizzy was pouring concrete to make the floor, and Roley was rolling it flat.

Scrambler and Scruffty chased each other until they found themselves in a beautiful valley, full of twisty paths and ditches.

"Wow!" exclaimed Scrambler. "Let's have an off-road race!"

"Ruff!" barked Scruffty, running ahead. The race was on!

The team had been busy all morning, and now the outside of the barn was completely finished.

"Excellent!" said Bob. "Now we need to build some shelves for Farmer Pickles to store things on."

"We'll need to concentrate," said Wendy. "It's a good thing Scruffty's not here!"

Scrambler and Scruffty were having the best time ever. They raced over rocks and through streams, getting very mucky.

"RUFF! RUFF! RUFF!" barked Scruffty, running through a hollow log.

"WHEEEEE!" cried Scrambler. "You can't catch me!"

At last, Scruffty landed in a big muddy puddle. Splash!

Back at the barn, work was finished. Bob and Wendy were having a rest and a cup of tea.

"I wonder where Scrambler's got to with Scruffty?" said Wendy, looking around.

Just then, Scrambler rumbled up. He was carrying something in his trailer.

"Scruffty's asleep!" said Scrambler.
"But I'm not tired." He tried not to yawn.

"See . . . dog-walking is a proper job," said Bob, lifting Scruffty from the trailer, "and you made a friend!"

Scruffty woke up and licked his new friend's nose. "Ruff!"

"Making friends is wicked!" Scrambler grinned happily.

THE END

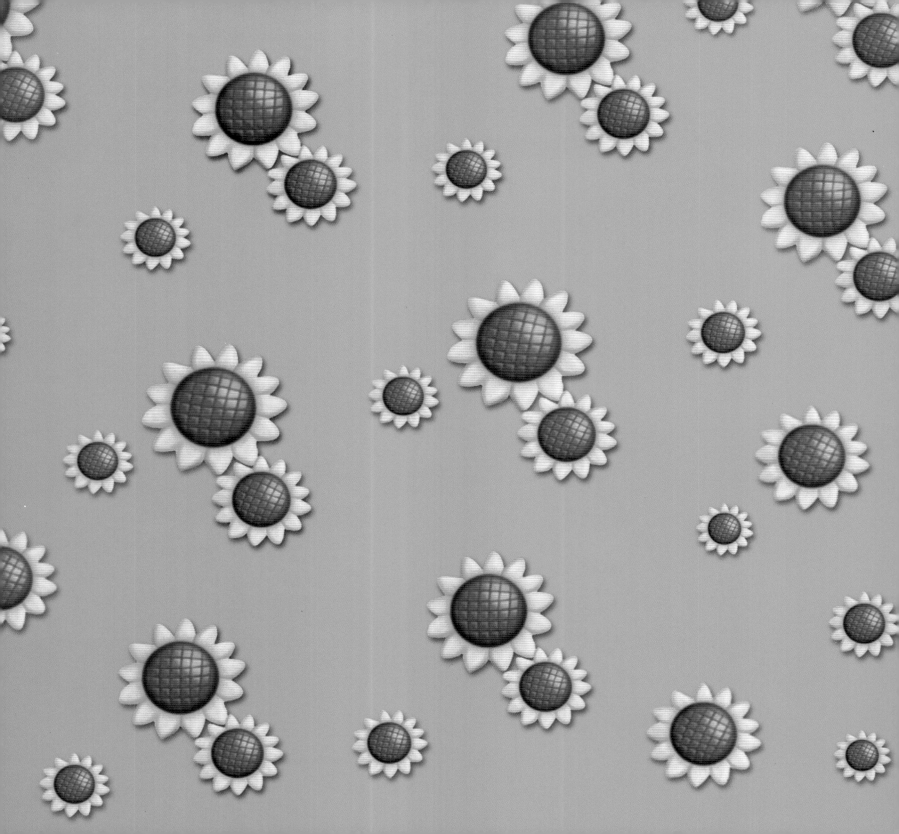

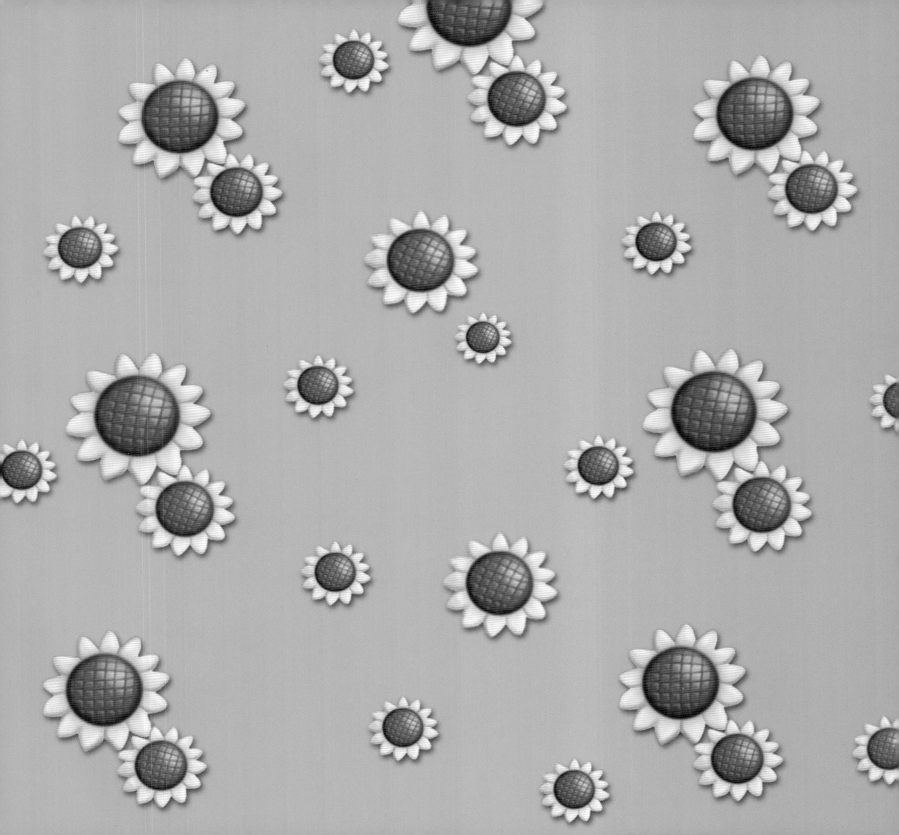

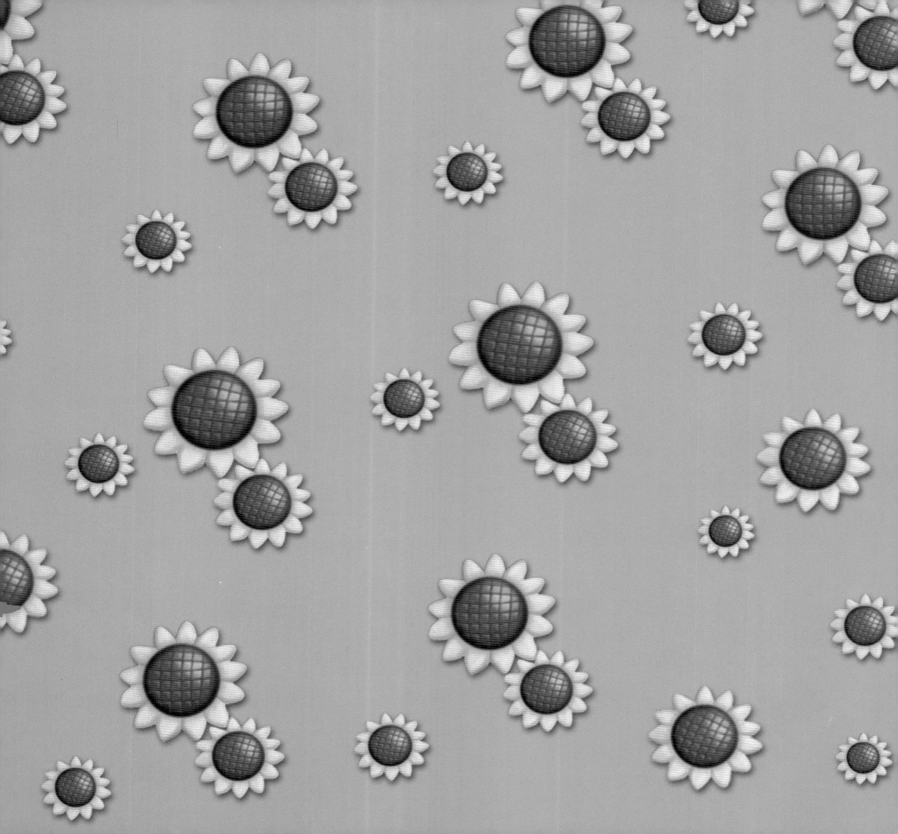